THE MILLS & BOON®
MODERN GIRL'S GUIDE TO

Turning Into Your Mother

HQ
An imprint of HarperCollinsPublishers Ltd.
1 London Bridge Street
London SE1 9GF

This hardback edition 2017

1
First published in Great Britain by
HQ, an imprint of HarperCollinsPublishers Ltd. 2017

A catalogue record for this book is
available from the British Library

ISBN: 978-0-00-824386-9

Printed and bound in Italy

Funny, feisty and feminist:
The Mills & Boon Modern Girl's Survival Guides.

Introduction

Motherhood is one of life's Big Miracles, right up there
at number seventeen – just above 'a nice bowl of crisps', and just
below 'those times you get a Kit-Kat but something went wrong
in the factory so the entire Kit-Kat is solid chocolate, no wafer!'

Unfortunately, another of the Big Miracles is the near-inevitability
of turning into your own mother, otherwise known as the
Circle Of Life, the same grim peril Elton sang about. You vowed you
wouldn't. You actively pursued the opposite life choices. And yet, here
you are, telling anyone who'll listen about your uncle's bowel problems,
and having an opinion on the weather.

Still convinced you're hip, with it, nothing like your old Ma? Well, this
handy guide will outline the many faces of motherhood. If they sound
familiar then, well, it's too late for you. But at least now you know
the signs, you can try to save your own daughter from a similar fate.
Let's face it, the next generation is screwed up enough as it is.

I myself have raised dozens of children over several marriages, because
I think it's important to have enough of them to be able to fully crew
a large yacht. And sure, I've mislaid a few – who hasn't? – but by
the ninth or tenth one I started to get the hang of it. I can even
remember some of their names on a good day. So I definitely know
what I'm talking about.

Yours as ever,
Ada

Art

Daphne's own mother never encouraged her creativity (which is probably why she's a miserable accountant not a millionaire with a wing in the Tate named after her), so she promised herself she'd never dismiss her own children's artistic efforts.

Still, there's a fine line between 'adorably precocious' and 'creepy enough that I'm going to start sleeping with one eye open'.

Bad Mother

<u>Ways In Which Karen's 'Support Network'</u>
<u>Has Made Karen Feel She Is Somehow</u>
<u>Not Quite Measuring Up As A Mother</u>

Her labour took a full three hours longer
than the other mums'

Her child drinks regular milk instead of Babyccinos

She hasn't even enrolled the kid for Chinese lessons
yet even though she's almost fourteen months old

Her child's first word was 'bums'

Breakfast in Bed

Yeah, I've held down a job yet somehow
still done *95%* of the childcare for the past
decade, but sure: breakfast in bed one day
a year and an entire ten-minute lie-in,
this definitely makes us even.

Costumes

Another thirty years of therapy and the triplets will probably be ready to forgive Simone for making their costumes for the school play out of old net curtains, food dye and Febreze.

But, given that Simone only found the letter in their book bag last night, she thinks she's done a pretty good job.

Cute

Jen had started off by hoping her daughter would stay away from gender-stereotyped toys and all that cutesy pink-pony-based stuff.

Now she just dreams of not waking up to a horrifying homunculus every morning.

Date Night

It is date night.

Letty has texted the babysitter nineteen times.

Fred has made a list in his head of all the
things at home that could spontaneously
go on fire (twelve).

They have reassured each other, once every
thirty seconds, that *everything will be fine*.

Letty and Fred have been out on the town
for a full twenty-six minutes.

Empty Nest

Jackie used to worry about the kids flying
the nest and the house feeling empty without them.

But it turns out that, thanks to today's crippling
house prices, that isn't so much of a problem.

Fantasies

Alternative Life Choices I Have Day-Dreamed About
Even Though Obviously I Love Being A Mother

Professional dilettante

Solving crimes with my fun elephant friend Jeff

Croissant ambassador, though I am not sure that's a thing

Sleeping for eighteen hours a day

In fact, just sleeping, oh my God

Girl

'Don't ever let the fact you're a girl make you think you can't be whatever you want to be!'

'Hang on, what? It never occurred to me that I *couldn't* be whatever I wanted to be. Why are you suddenly telling me that? Mum? Is there something bad I need to know? What have you been hiding?'

'Look, forget I said anything.'

Gran

It was the first time she'd left the baby with Gran, but Elspeth had provided a comprehensive list of instructions, so, really - what was the worst that could happen?

Harsh Truth

Mummy, you were my best friend
until I actually got friends.

Holidays

Val had sorted the itinerary, packed the snacks,
made sure the kids had their bathing suits,
and bought the tickets to the waterpark.

Kevin had one job.

This was not that job.

Internet

Bad Advice I Have Received From A Certain Online
Forum Devoted To Motherhood

Give them only pickled eggs until the age of six

Dip a teething baby in brandy

No bright lights, never get them wet,
never feed them after midnight

Juggling

Michelle, 32, got herself a new outfit, because she felt it was important to make a big impression on the CEO at the company AGM.

Archie, 6 months, felt it was important to make a big impression on Michelle's outfit about five minutes before she was due to set off.

Keep Off

Things I Say To Stop Random Strangers
Petting My Baby

'Go ahead, but he's at that bitey stage –
took a man's finger clean off the other day'

'He has a touch of the plague right now,
but nothing to worry about'

'Funnily enough, he's actually full of bees'

'You pet it you own it'

Let it Go

This piano has been in Mildred's family
for over one hundred years.

It once sat in the corner of her great,
great grandparents' pub.

It has survived two world wars.

But if Mildred hears so much as the opening bars
one more time then the bloody thing is going
on freecycle.

Logistics

It has taken five months of solid planning,
but the complexities of taking the kids to the local
park for half an hour have almost been worked out.

Mother & Baby Cinema

Maybe, if you stuff *enough* popcorn into your face, a room full of toddlers screaming their way through a 10am showing of *Ghostbusters* can become semi-bearable.

Janine is going to give it her best shot, anyhow.

Mummy's Special Calpol

The best thing about our former Prime Minister
forgetting his kid in the pub is that almost
anything Elaine does can now be passed
off as 'statesmanlike'.

Naughty Step

Super Nanny fails to mention what to do when your kids are so annoying that you run out of stairs.

Not Again

A List Of Terrible Mother's Day Gifts I Have Received

Unflattering picture of my face made
out of pasta and glue

'Platinum edition' dishwasher tablets

A book about worms even though I have never
expressed any interest in worms

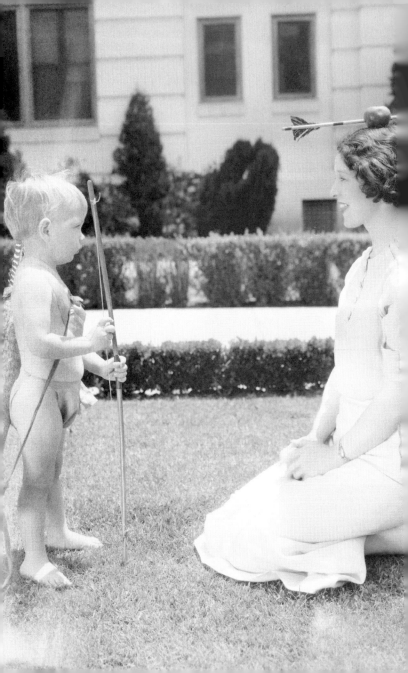

Ominous

We need to talk about Kevin and this whole 'archery' fad.

Passwords

Somehow Ned got hold of the iPad and the credit card and, long story short, we've now got five hundred pints of milk to get through.

Questions

Why don't you have a willy?

Can I keep this dust ball as a pet?

When are you going to die?

Why are you a poo poo head?

Can I live with Peppa Pig?

What is the *point* of you, mummy?

Rainy Day

Doris reckons she has ten minutes before they realise that the Super Fun Apple Game is just a scheme to shut them up, but she's going to savour every blissful silent second.

Revenge

Jane's mother is refusing to let her play
with the boy next door until she finishes
her maths homework.

In exactly fifteen years Jane will bring home Darren,
an unemployed musician with a Harley and several
questionable tattoos, and this day will finally
be avenged.

School Gates

At some point the unspoken one-upmanship with the other mums had degenerated into a weird hat-based arms race, and none of them quite knew how it had happened.

Signs

<u>Signs You're Turning Into Your Mother:</u>

The Ordinance Survey map of lines under your eyes

A genuinely heartfelt interest in the weather

You bought a whole house for about ten quid
in 1972, yet now enjoy moaning about how
'this generation are spoilt with their iPhones'

You get excited when *Countryfile* runs a segment
about a new kind of vegetable

Tantrums

You are trying to murder me with sweet corn.

I hate you.

I hate sweet corn.

Why do you want me to die?

Because I will die if I have to eat sweet corn,
that's how much I hate it.

A kid in California divorced their parents because
of having to eat sweet corn. Did you know that?
I DECLARE A CITIZEN'S DIVORCE.

Translating

Did you brush your hair?

*I know you have brushed your hair, I just
don't like the way you've brushed it.*

Well, you have to make your own mistakes.

I told you so.

What a lovely surprise to hear from you.

*It's been so long since you called that I thought
you were dead. Why would you treat your poor dear
mum this way? It's a wonder I've not died myself
– of a broken heart. And to think I carried you for
nine months. If I'd not had kids I could have been
a ballerina, oh, the opportunities I gave up for you.*

Unqualified

Susan has just had the terrifying epiphany that,
unlike driving a car or buying cigarettes or rewiring
a house, they let literally *anyone* be a mother.

Even *estate agents* probably have to pass a test
of some kind, thinks Susan, so how the hell
is it possible that she's wound up in this situation?

Unsuitable Role Models

I know your mother tells you to stay away
from boys and gin.

But your old Auntie Ada has been married eight
times, sometimes to two guys at once, and she
makes her own gin in an illegal distillery hidden
in the basement.

And, let me tell you, neither of those things
ever did her any harm.

Very Special Friend

Four hours putting up 'Missing Toy' posters
and a trek round a dozen shops to find another
Mister Cloppy after the original Mister Cloppy
got left on a train, but even after bidding £220
for an identical Mr Cloppy on eBay I've still
somehow failed as a mother, because apparently
the original Mr Cloppy is *irreplaceable.*

What's in Mum's Handbag

400 baby wipes

½ a smooshed banana

Valium

Sunglasses to hide the effects of all the Valium

Sun Maid raisins scattered like mouse droppings,
or possibly just mouse droppings

A photo of an ex-boyfriend who she thinks
might have been the one

A baby sock with sick on it

Wine

Phyllis is doing the family shop.

'Coffee' is her code for 'Wine'.

'Milk' is also her code for Wine.

'Lettuce' is definitely code for Wine.

The 'Butter' is actual butter, to have with the wine.

****-ing hell

Not for the first time, Delia found herself thinking about how the Harp Seal abandons its offspring to fend for themselves after just three weeks.

Yuck

A good way to get the kids to finally go to bed is to start snogging in front of them, because they will regard this as unforgivably gross.

Bill and Angela find that using a magnifying glass to provide an unwanted close-up of the action is extra effective.

The hat is just some Cumberbatch-themed role-play stuff they're trying out.

Zzzzzz

'No, dear, tell me again about how a T-Rex
could never beat a Storm-Trooper.'

About Ada Adverse

Ada has been married eight times, including, on one occasion in the early 90's, to a rock - a full twenty years, you'll note, before Tracy Emin came up with the same idea. Unlucky in love, all of Ada's partners have died in tragic circumstances, mostly unexplained fires.

Ada's interests include life insurance policies, petrol and topical poisons.

About Mills & Boon®

Since 1908, Mills & Boon® have been a girl's best friend.

We've seen a lot change in the years since: enjoying sex as a woman is now not only officially fine but actively encouraged, dry shampoo has revolutionised our lives and, best of all, we've come full circle on gin.

But being a woman still has its challenges. We're under-paid, exhaustingly objectified, and under-represented at top tables. We work for free from 19th November, and our life-choices are scrutinised and forever found lacking. Plus: PMS; unsolicited d*ck pics; the price of tights.

Sometimes, a girl just needs a break.
And, for a century, that's where we've come in.

So, to celebrate one hundred years of wisdom (or at least a lot of fun), we've produced these handy A-Zs: funny, feisty, feminist guides to help the modern girl get through the day.

We can't promise an end to the bullsh*t.
But we can offer some light relief along the way.

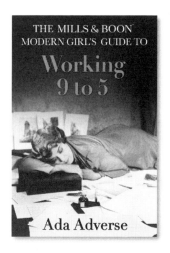

THE MILLS & BOON
MODERN GIRL'S GUIDE TO

Working
9 to 5

Ada Adverse

THE MILLS & BOON
MODERN GIRL'S GUIDE TO

Happy
Hour

Ada Adverse

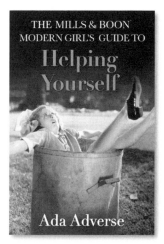

THE MILLS & BOON
MODERN GIRL'S GUIDE TO

Helping
Yourself

Ada Adverse

THE MILLS & BOON
MODERN GIRL'S GUIDE TO

Happy
Endings

Ada Adverse

#ModernGirls